Library of Congress Control Number: 2016952346
ISBN 978-0-06-264076-5

Typography by Brenda E. Angelilli
17 18 19 20 21   SCP   10 9 8 7 6 5 4 3 2 1
❖
First Edition

I Am the Walrus

adapted by Anne Lamb
based on a story written by Josh Wakely
Beat Bugs created by Josh Wakely

HARPER FESTIVAL
An Imprint of HarperCollinsPublishers

This is the story of how the Beat Bugs first met Walter Walrus.

Walter Walrus lived in the old garden next door. Until one day, big trucks came in and suddenly his home wasn't safe for a squishy slug anymore. The trucks rumbled everywhere, and more than once, Walter almost got run over!

So Walter packed up his stuff in a small box and left his old garden behind. He knew he had to find a new home—and quickly!

Walter slipped through a crack in a tall fence and discovered on the other side a magnificent new garden where the grass grew thick and tall. It was Beat Bugs Village, and Walter found lots of bugs living happily.

Walter decided Beat Bugs Village would be the perfect place for a new home!

"Houses are hard to come by in this neighborhood," said a raspy voice behind him. Walter spun around and saw a sleazy cockroach grinning at him.

"But you're a lucky slug," Geoff the Cockroach said. It turned out there was still one place available for Walter to live.

The roach led Walter over to a gloomy corner of the village. He pointed to a dirty deflated basketball.

"I'm sure you're gonna love it here!" Geoff chuckled and scuttled away.

Walter looked uncertainly at the ball. It was covered in moss and grime. It needed a lot of work, but it would have to do.

Walter was happy to have a new home, but he was very lonely.
"I don't have any friends. Not one. Not a single slug or bug."
Walter sighed.
   He had lots of friends in his old garden, but now he didn't
know anyone.

To keep from being too lonely, Walter focused on fixing up the inside of his house.

Until one day he heard laughter and shouting coming from outside. He looked out his window and saw a group of bugs playing in the village green.

"I will go out and find some new friends," Walter decided. He gathered up all his courage and went to meet the bugs in his new neighborhood.

But as he approached the group, trash suddenly dropped on Walter from the big people's house at the edge of the garden. An egg smashed all over him!

He wound up dripping with gooey egg! The shell covered his head! He couldn't see a thing. Walter stumbled and bumbled around.

The Beat Bugs stopped playing and stared at Walter.

"What is that?" asked Buzz the Fruit Fly.

"I think it's an eggman," replied Crick the Cricket.

"No, I'm not! I'm— My name—" Walter flapped his hands around and tried to explain, but his voice was muffled by the eggshell.

The Beat Bugs couldn't hear Walter. When he tried to move closer to them, the eggshell began to crack and fall apart. *Good*, Walter thought. He might be a bit gooey, but at least he wasn't trapped in an egg anymore. Finally, he could introduce himself properly!

"It looks like he might explode," Kumi the Ladybug yelled. "Quick, everyone hide!"

"I don't think he's safe!" Jay the Beetle said.

The Beat Bugs ran and hid from Walter. This was certainly not going as Walter had planned.

Finally, Walter tugged the last of the eggshell off his head. He saw the Beat Bugs running away and hiding from him. He couldn't believe what had happened. Walter was so sad and embarrassed that he hurried straight home. He was sure now he'd never make any new friends.

Walter stared for a long time at his picture of his beloved great uncle Tusk. Great Uncle Tusk had been a fabulous performer, despite having stage fright. Walter always admired him for that. "I need to find some courage," he told himself.

Then Walter remembered something his uncle told him long ago when he was just a little slugling.

"You have to grab life by the tusks and declare who you are to the world! Whatever is unique about you is the thing that is the most wonderful about you," Great Uncle Tusk had told Walter.

He also told Walter, "Always be yourself.
Always be brave, which is hard sometimes.
But you are Walter Walrus. Remember, if you believe
in who you are, people will love you!"

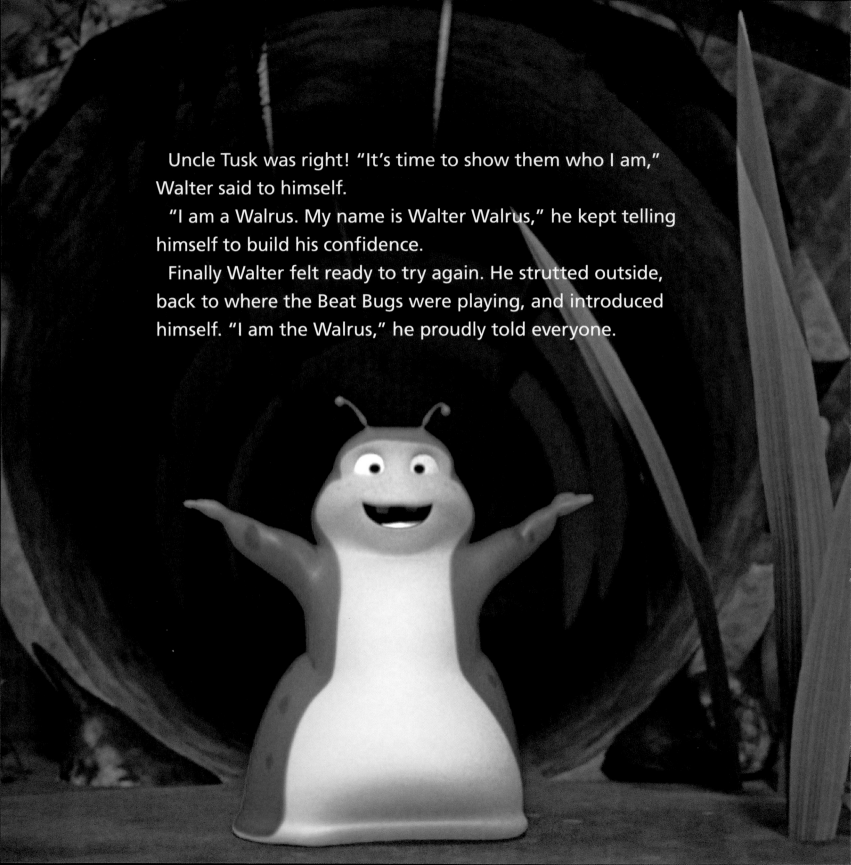

Uncle Tusk was right! "It's time to show them who I am," Walter said to himself.

"I am a Walrus. My name is Walter Walrus," he kept telling himself to build his confidence.

Finally Walter felt ready to try again. He strutted outside, back to where the Beat Bugs were playing, and introduced himself. "I am the Walrus," he proudly told everyone.

Walter shared his love of singing and dancing with the Beat Bugs
by singing his favorite song while wiggling and jiggling his squish.
The Beat Bugs realized Walter looked like he'd be a lot of fun to play with!

To show them that he likes to be silly, Walter picked up the eggshell
and put it on his head like a hat.
"I am the eggman," he joked. The Beat Bugs busted up laughing.

Then the Beat Bugs danced and laughed and clapped along with Walter's song. They even began to sing with him.

Walter had done it. Just by being himself, Walter had made new friends.

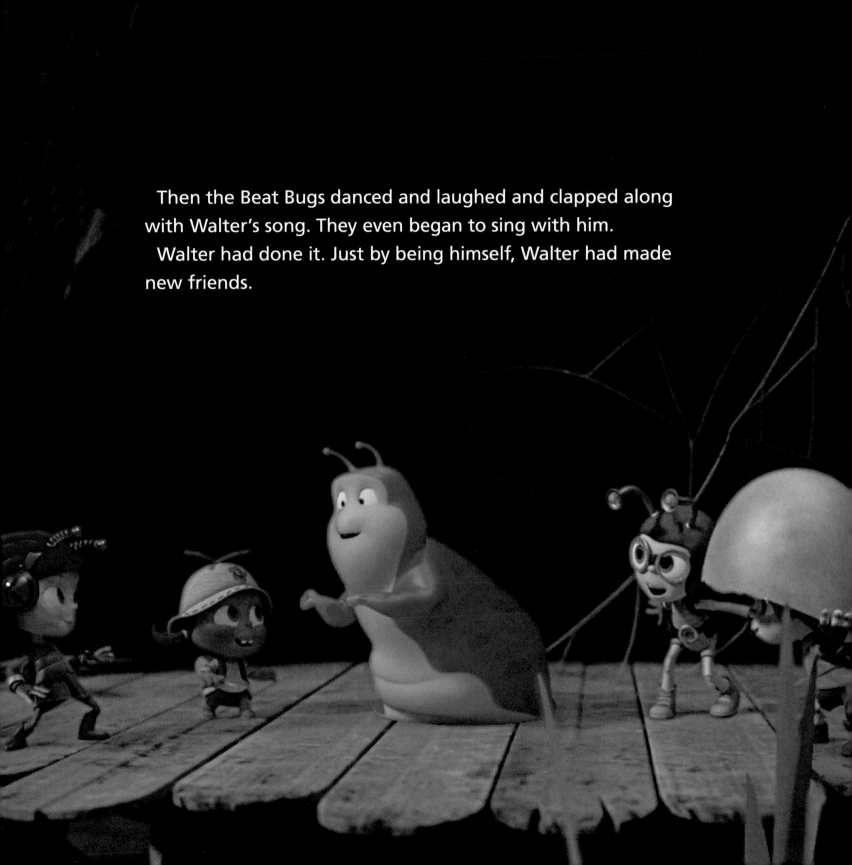

Kumi, Jay, Crick, and Buzz officially welcomed Walter to the neighborhood and to their group. They even helped clean and fix their new friend's house.

When Walter saw how his new friends had helped him decorate his house, he was so happy he nearly burst into tears of joy.

"Oh my. It's so nice to have friends," he said. "It's group-hug time!"

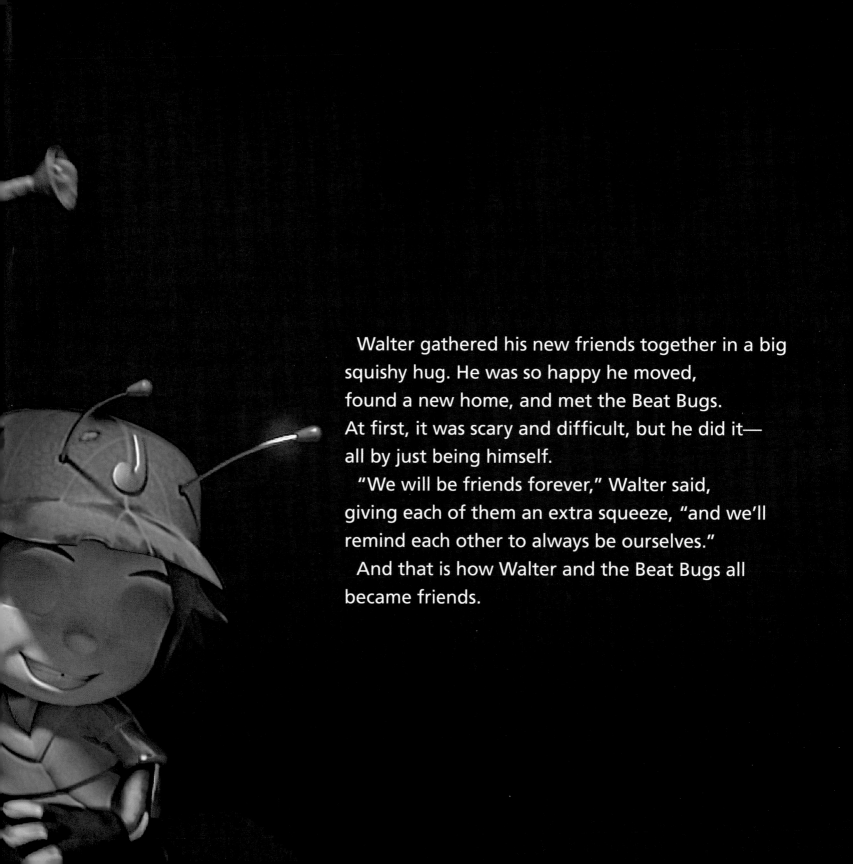

Walter gathered his new friends together in a big squishy hug. He was so happy he moved, found a new home, and met the Beat Bugs. At first, it was scary and difficult, but he did it—all by just being himself.

"We will be friends forever," Walter said, giving each of them an extra squeeze, "and we'll remind each other to always be ourselves."

And that is how Walter and the Beat Bugs all became friends.

It's not over until Walter sings— join him!

"I Am the Walrus" lyrics

Written by John Lennon/Paul McCartney

I am he as you are he
As you are me and we are all together.

I am the eggman, they are the eggmen,
I am the walrus.
Goo goo g'joob, goo goo g'joob.

See how they fly like Lucy in the sky,
See how they run, I'm crying.
I'm crying,
I'm crying,
I'm crying.

I am the eggman, they are the eggmen,
I am the walrus.
Goo goo g'joob, goo goo g'joob.
Goo goo g'joob, goo goo g'joob.

Sitting in an English garden, waiting for the sun.
If the sun don't come, you get a tan
From standing in the English rain.

I am the eggman, they are the eggmen,
I am the walrus.
Goo goo g'joob, goo goo g'joob.

I am the eggman, they are the eggmen,
I am the walrus.
Goo goo g'joob, goo goo g'joob.
Goo goo g'joob, goo goo g'joob.

Joob-a, joob-a, joob-a, joob-a
×18